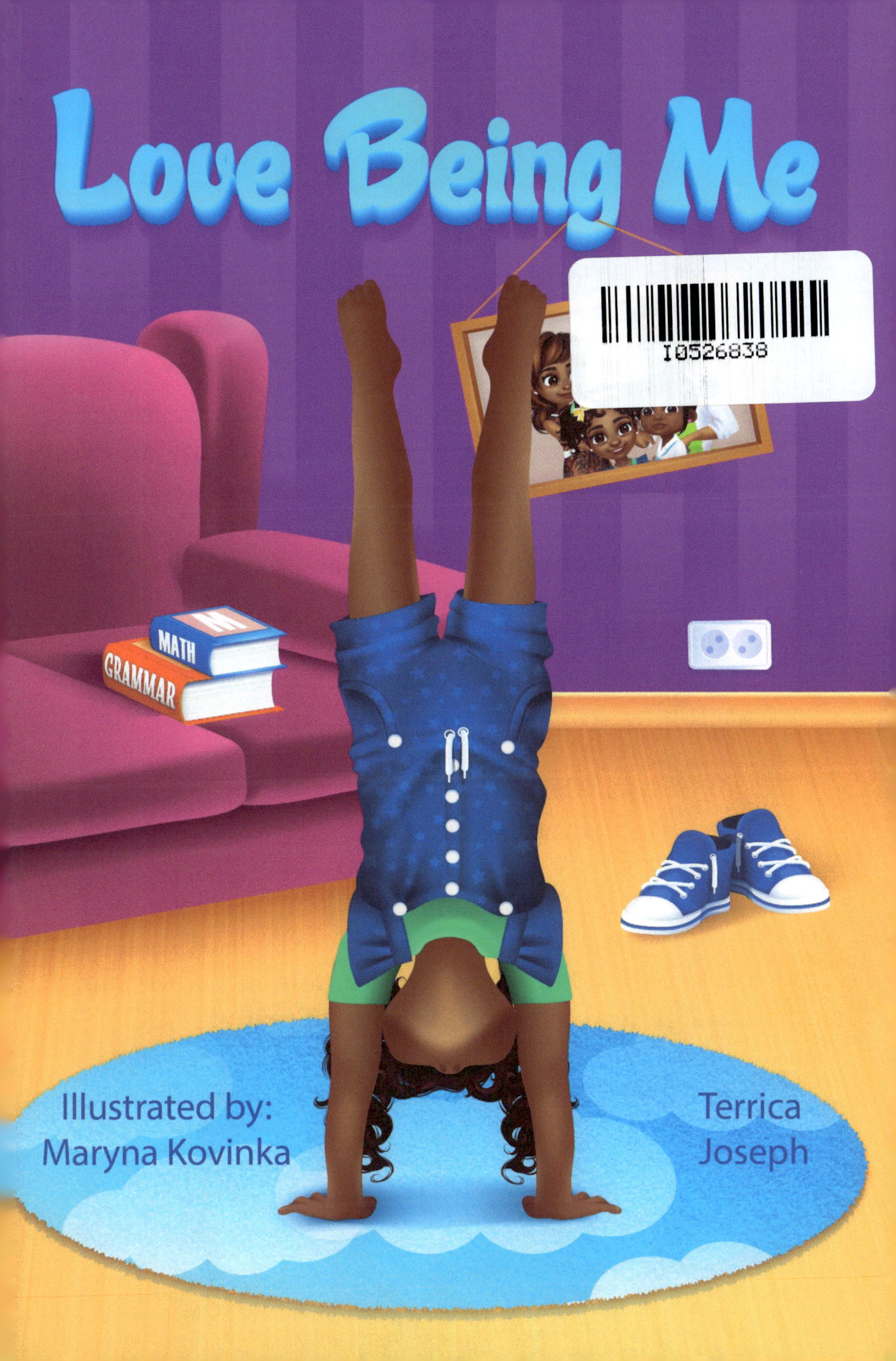

Love Being Me
MATH
GRAMMAR
Illustrated by:
Maryna Kovinka
Terrica
Joseph

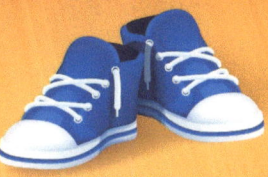

Fruit Springs, LLC

Omaha, Nebraska

ISBN 978-1-970016-27-7 (Hardcover Ed)
ISBN 978-1-970016-28-4 (Paperback Ed)
Cataloging-in-Publication date on file with the
publisher.

Published by Fruit Springs, LLC
17330 W Center Rd Ste. 110-342
Omaha, NE 68130

Illustrated by: Maryna Kovinka, Alena Katomina
Design and production: Fruit Springs, LLC

Printed in the United States of America
10 9 8 7 6 5 4 3 2 1

Dedication

To my lovely niece Cassie. You were loved and approved before you were sent!

It was an early morning. Cassie stretched her arms out to feel the morning mist. Closing her eyes, she imagined herself flying through the air. Cassie was an adventurer and dreamed of doing amazing things. Sometimes she even pretended to be a bird, flying over the neighborhood.

4

Slowly opening the door, her sister Isabel sneaked
inside the room.
"Cassie, what are you doing?" asked Isabel.
"I'm just feeling the air. What are you wearing?"
"It's my doctor's coat. I may be a doctor someday."
"The thought of you trying to bandage me up is
terrifying," Cassie replied.

"Stick out your tongue. Let me have a look in there," demanded Isabel.

"Not a chance," said Cassie as she grabbed her backpack and walked toward the door.

Cassie thought Isabel might be on-to something, but maybe not. Her sister wanted to be a police officer just last week.

Cassie giggled. "What are you going to be tomorrow, a chef? I don't know if our kitchen will survive."

"How will I know what I'm good at or who I can be if I don't try? Do you know what you want to be?" asked Isabel.

"I don't know who I'll be, but I'm sure I'll figure it out."

"Well, you can always be my guinea pig."

"Oh brother, not even in your dreams," said Cassie as she raced out to the school bus.

As she stepped off the bus, Cassie heard a loud shriek.
It was her best friend, Christine.
"Over here. Over here!" yelled Isabel.
"What's going on?" Cassie asked.
"It's here. It's here!" she replied.
"What's here?"
"The butterfly exhibit in the library. We have to go see them," Christine squealed.

"I thought you were being chased by wild spiders," said
Cassie.
"No, silly. I'm just excited about the butterflies," said
Christine.
The friends loved watching butterflies but were never
able to get close enough to see all their colors. This was
their only chance to examine the butterflies up close.
The girls rushed to the library.

"Welcome to the amazing exhibit," said Mrs. Green.
"Wow. It really is amazing," said Christine.
"Oh, look! It's a monarch butterfly. It's beautiful. Did you know that it can take four weeks for them to come out of their chrysalis?" asked Cassie.
"You seem to know a great deal about butterflies."
"She knows the name of nearly every butterfly and where they like to hide. She's a butterfly genius," replied Christine.

"Are you sure you don't want to be a butterfly researcher when you grow up?" asked Mrs. Green.
"I like butterflies, but I'm not sure I want to be a researcher," Cassie replied.
"I'm sure you'll figure it out. Now, off to class. You don't want to be late," said Mrs. Green.
They took another look at the butterflies and hurried to class.

Talent show

"Good morning class, I have great news. We are hosting another talent show," said Mrs. Moon.
"When?" the students asked.
"The show will be tomorrow after lunch. I want you all to enter and share your talents." After a brief moment of silence, the class erupted in cheers.

Cassie looked around in horror. Talent shows were fun but just thinking of them made her heart pound. Cassie had pretended to be a teacher, an astronaut and a singer, but things never went the way she'd planned, and she never acted in front of others.

"Christine, I'm not sure about this talent show. I've tried dancing, singing and magic tricks. I don't know if I'm good at anything. Maybe I'll just read a book," said Cassie.

"At least you can whistle. Math is my only talent," said Christine.

"I like singing, but we all know how that turned out the last time."

"Kids were covering their ears. They said it sounded like I was scratching my nails on a chalkboard." Both girls laughed at the memory.

"Maybe you should do something else," Christine suggested.

"What am I going to do? I'm not good at everything, but I must be good at something. I just don't know what it is."

Cassie thought nervously about the talent show, but her classmates were excited.
She had many talents, but she didn't think so. She was smart, funny and creative, but most of all she was a good friend to everyone in school. Her thoughts were interrupted by Mrs. Moon's call for her attention to the board.
"Class, let's begin our lesson. Cassie, complete the equation, 4 X 4, equals," said Mrs. Moon.
"4 X 4=15," said Cassie.

Roger laughed. "Are you good at anything?"

"Hey, that's not nice," said Cassie.

"Class, remember only kind and encouraging words. Try again, Cassie."

"Hmm, I got it. 4X4 equals 16!" Cassie exclaimed.

"Great job," said Mrs. Moon.

"I knew I could do it," whispered Cassie as she took her seat.

News of the talent show had spread throughout the
school. All the students were talking about their talents
and what they were going to do. Cassie still didn't
know her talent or who she wanted to be. It was a
long school day for Cassie, and she rushed home after
school to tell her mom about the big show.

"Mom, Mom," Cassie called.

"In here! What's wrong? You sound like you have
bad news."

"There's a talent show, but I'm not sure that I have a talent," said Cassie with a frown on her face.
"Sure you do," Mom replied.
"I wish I knew what my talents are."
"A talent can be something you're good at or just enjoy doing. You have lots of interests and can do many things."
"I sure hope so," said Cassie.

19

Cassie sat in her room and tried to think about her talents. She decided to juggle her balls to help her think. It had always worked before. This time she used three balls instead of the normal two. She tossed them around until it was time for dinner.

"Mom, I can't think of anything," said Cassie.
"Don't give up. I'm sure you'll think of something," her mother said.
"I've tried being everyone else and everything I could think of. Maybe it's time to try something else," Cassie replied.
Cassie finished her dinner and went back to her room.

"Maybe I can find my talent while doing a handstand,"
said Cassie.
She stood on her hands and began walking around the
room, but it didn't work.

She tried walking with a book on her head and tried hula hooping on one foot, but that didn't work either. Soon it was time for bed, and Cassie fell asleep thinking about the big talent show.

23

The next day, Cassie thought of staying in bed, but the smell of her dad's pancakes made her rush to breakfast. "Dad, I tried but I couldn't find my talent," said Cassie. "You can blow the biggest bubbles, say your ABC's backwards, sing, and ride your bike."

"Those are talents," her dad said.
"That's just me being myself. Do you really mean those are talents?"
"Yes, they are. You are one of a kind and have your own way of doing things. It's what makes you special."
"Maybe I do have talents," Cassie said in surprise.
She quickly ate her pancakes and went to school.

When class began, Mrs. Moon asked each student about their talents. The students were excited to tell her and could hardly wait their turn. Cassie listened all morning to her friends talk about their talents, but she decided to keep hers a secret. When it was time for lunch, Mrs. Moon walked the class to the cafeteria and wished them all good luck. They ate their food but no one played during recess. They were all practicing for the show.

Mrs. Moon blew the whistle and called everyone to the cafeteria to begin the show. Many were still practicing, but some still didn't have a talent. Cassie encouraged her friends.

"You all have talents. Just do what you like and it will be fine," said Cassie.

"It's time to begin. Everyone take your seats," said Mrs. Moon.

One by one each student went up to display a talent. Roger did a magic trick, Lily performed ballet and Christine shared her math skills. They all had talents that showed just how special they were, and they showed it bravely. Cassie decided to perform last.

She walked on stage and cleared her throat. "Hello, everyone, I'm Cassie and my talent is being Cassie."
She took a deep breath and began singing and dancing happily around the stage. She threw paper hearts while she twirled and hugged herself while she sang. It was beautiful. She finished with a bow and everyone cheered.

Mrs. Moon collected the votes and went on stage to announce the winner. The students sat on the edge of their seats.

"You all did a wonderful job. We've counted the votes, and the winner of today's talent show is…Cassie!"

They all cheered. Everyone liked Cassie's song and dance, but most of all they liked the fact that Cassie was just being herself.

Cassie accepted her award and spoke to her friends.
"When I grow up, I want to be happy with who I am.
Being myself is a talent, and that means you all have a
special talent, too, just by being yourselves. We are all
unique and are the best at being ourselves. No one else
can do it but you."

31